Dear Parent:
Your child's love of reading starts here!

Every child learns to read in a different way and at his or her own speed. Some go back and forth between reading levels and read favorite books again and again. Others read through each level in order. You can help your young reader improve and become more confident by encouraging his or her own interests and abilities. From books your child reads with you to the first books he or she reads alone, there are I Can Read Books for every stage of reading:

SHARED READING
Basic language, word repetition, and whimsical illustrations, ideal for sharing with your emergent reader

BEGINNING READING
Short sentences, familiar words, and simple concepts for children eager to read on their own

READING WITH HELP
Engaging stories, longer sentences, and language play for developing readers

READING ALONE
Complex plots, challenging vocabulary, and high-interest topics for the independent reader

I Can Read Books have introduced children to the joy of reading since 1957. Featuring award-winning authors and illustrators and a fabulous cast of beloved characters, I Can Read Books set the standard for beginning readers.

A lifetime of discovery begins with the magical words "I Can Read!"

*Visit www.icanread.com for information
on enriching your child's reading experience.*

**Visit www.zonderkidz.com/icanread for more faith-based
I Can Read! titles from Zonderkidz.**

ZONDERKIDZ

I Can Read Fantastic Fiona
Copyright © 2021 by Zondervan
Illustrations: © 2021 by Zondervan

An **I Can Read Book**

Requests for information should be addressed to:
Zonderkidz, *3900 Sparks Drive SE, Grand Rapids, Michigan 49546*

Softcover ISBN 978-0-310-77100-5
Hardcover ISBN 978-0-310-77101-2
Ebook ISBN 978-0-310-77102-9

Editor: Mary Hassinger
Art direction and design: Cindy Davis
Content Contributor: Katelyn VanKooten

I Can Read® and I Can Read Book® are trademarks of HarperCollins Publishers.

Printed in United States of America

21 22 23 24 25 26 /LSCC/ 15 14 13 12 11 10 9 8 7 6 5 4 3 2 1

Fantastic Fiona

New York Times Bestselling Illustrator
Richard Cowdrey
and Donald Wu

Fiona loved her home.

The zoo was a happy place.

Many special animals lived there.
"Am I special too?" she wondered.

Fiona found Kris the cheetah.

"What makes you special?"
Fiona asked.

"I run very fast," Kris said.

"Watch!"

Kris raced around.

Fiona huffed and puffed
behind her.

"That is special!" she said.

Nearby, the gorillas played.

Fiona joined them.

Gorillas laughed and smiled.

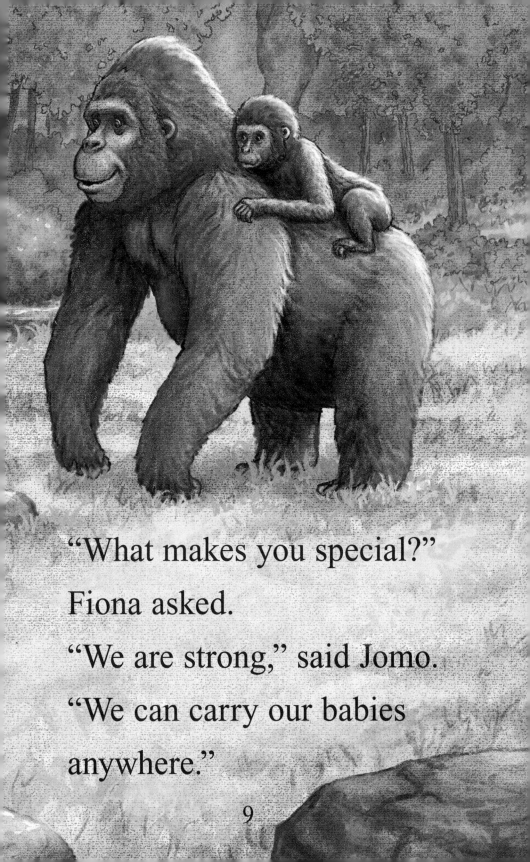

"What makes you special?"
Fiona asked.

"We are strong," said Jomo.

"We can carry our babies
anywhere."

Fiona tried to lift a baby.

She could not do it.

"I am not very strong yet," she said.

"See you later."

Fiona heard music.

The wolves were singing a song,

howling together very loud.

"You sound so good!" Fiona said.

"I want to try."

She took a deep breath …

… and bellowed!

Fiona did not sound like the wolves.

"I'm not a singer," Fiona said.

"What else could I do?"

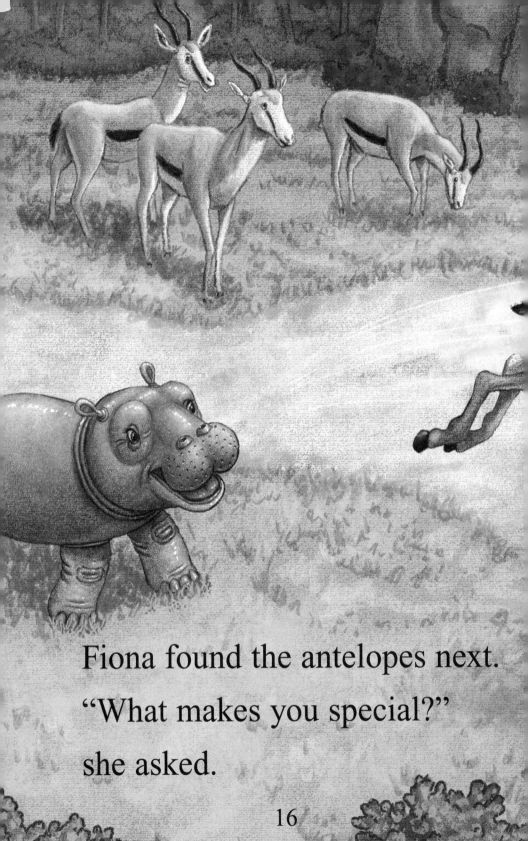

Fiona found the antelopes next.
"What makes you special?"
she asked.

"Watch this!" they said.

They jumped one by one.

They sprang high in the air.

One leaped over a bush.

"Wow!" said Fiona.

"Try it!" said the antelope.

"I've got this!" Fiona said.

She ran toward the bush.

She jumped as high as she could.

Fiona did not jump over the bush.

"I'll try something else," she said.

"I'm not a good jumper."

Fiona found the monkeys.

They climbed up and down the trees.

They swung from branch to branch.

"I've got this!" said Fiona.

Fiona tried to climb a tree.

She tried again and again.

"I can't climb," she said.

"What can I do that is special?"

Fiona was stumped.

She was not tall like the giraffes.

Or colorful like the parrots.

She could not hear like the foxes.

Or fly like the eagles.

Kris the cheetah came running by.
"What's wrong, Fiona?" asked Kris.

"I can't do anything special,"
Fiona said.
"I can't jump or climb or sing,"
Fiona said.

"Everyone is special!" said Kris.

Soon, other animals joined them.

"Yes, Fiona! You are kind,"
said Jomo.

"You play with us!" said the babies.

"You say nice things," said a wolf.

"You make your friends happy."

"You are brave," said an antelope.

"You try new things," said a monkey.

"Even if they are hard or scary."

Fiona smiled.

"You all think I am special?"

"More than special!" said Kris.

"You are fantastic!
Fantastic Fiona!"
Fiona wiggled her ears.
She really was fantastic!